I'll Wait, Mr. Panda

Yo voy a esperar, Sr. Panda

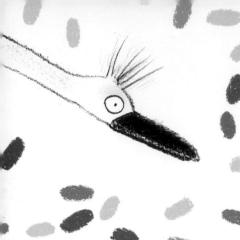

A papá

Originally published in English in Great Britain by Hodder Children's Books,
an imprint of Hachette Children's Group, as *I'll Wait, Mr. Panda*

Translated by Eida de la Vega

ISBN 978-1-338-11415-7

10 9 8 7 6 5 4 3 2 1   17 18 19 20 21

Printed in the U.S.A.   08
First Scholastic Spanish printing 2017

I'll Wait, Mr. Panda

Yo voy a esperar, Sr. Panda

Steve Antony

SCHOLASTIC INC.

What are
you making,
Mr. Panda?

¿Qué estás
haciendo,
Sr. Panda?

Wait and see. It's a surprise.
Espera y verás. Es una sorpresa.

No, I will not wait.
Good-bye.

No, no voy a esperar.
Adiós.

I'll wait, Mr. Panda.

Yo voy a esperar, Sr. Panda.

Are you
making cookies,
Mr. Panda?

¿Estás haciendo
galletitas,
Sr. Panda?

Wait and see. It's a surprise.

Espera y verás. Es una sorpresa.

No, waiting
is too hard.
Good-bye.

No, esperar es
muy difícil.
Adiós.

I'll wait, Mr. Panda.

Yo voy a esperar, Sr. Panda.

No,
I'm done
waiting.

No,
me cansé
de esperar.

Is it ready yet, Mr. Panda?

¿Ya está listo, Sr. Panda?

No, wait here.

No, espera aquí.

I don't like waiting.
No me gusta esperar.

Good-bye.

Adiós.

I'll wait, Mr. Panda!

¡Yo voy a esperar, Sr. Panda!

I'm waiting, Mr. Panda.

Estoy esperando, Sr. Panda.

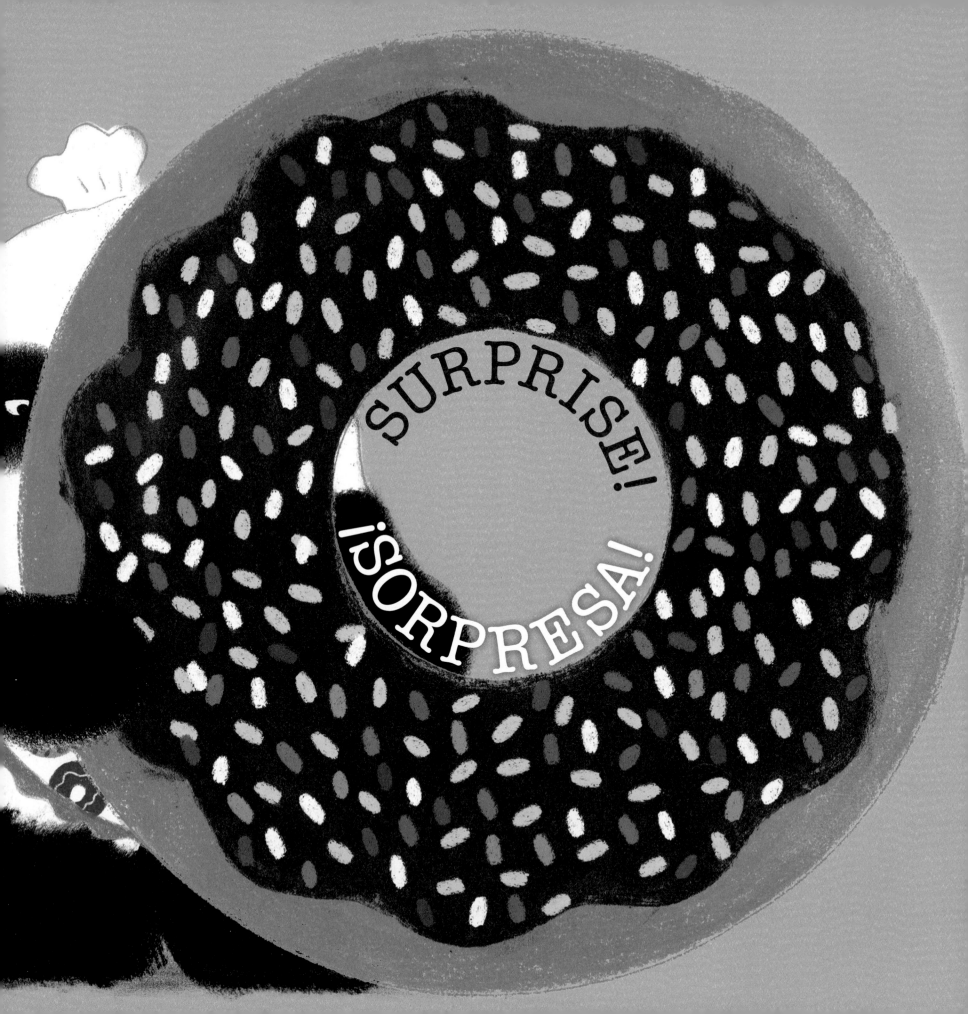

WOW! That was worth the wait.

¡CARAMBA! Valió la pena esperar.

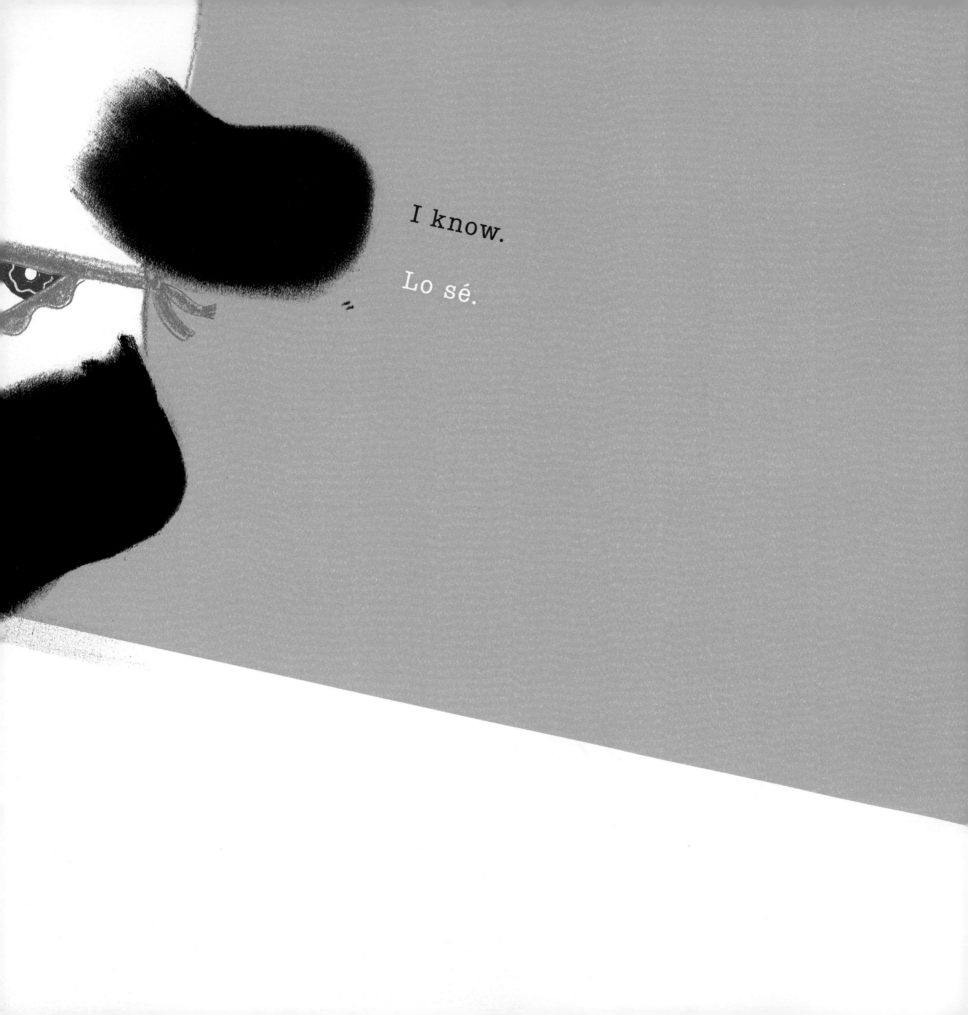

I know.

Lo sé.

Thank you, Mr. Panda. I can't wait to eat it!

Gracias, Sr. Panda. ¡No voy a esperar para comérmela!